Simon

SIMON AND MAGGIE ON THE LANDING

Simon

Irish Boy Encounters New Orleans

Laura Sheerin Gaus with illustrations by
Katherine Harman Harding

Writers Club Press
San Jose New York Lincoln Shanghai

Simon
Irish Boy Encounters New Orleans

Writers Club Press
an imprint of iUniverse.com, Inc.

For information address:
iUniverse.com, Inc.
5220 S 16th, Ste. 200
Lincoln, NE 68512
www.iuniverse.com

Illustrated by Katherine Harman Harding

ISBN: 0-595-17694-1

Printed in the United States of America

For
Joe, Arthur, Ann, Edward, Paul and William

Contents

List of Illustrations

Preface

This is a work of fiction woven around an actual historical event. It's the tale of how my Irish ancestors left Dublin for New Orleans and ended up in Indiana. Simon died before I was born, but he was my grandfather, so I have known the essentials of this story all my life. It was only when I gained possession of some old family scrapbooks, however, that I developed a need to write about it. This is just a beginning…I have enjoyed it. I hope you, the readers, will too.

Laura Sheerin Gaus

Acknowledgments

My thanks to:

Barbara Shoup, Susan Neville and all my fellow-participants at the Indiana University Writers Conference who insisted I should write this book.

Angela Pneuman, who provided valuable assistance at the beginning of the project.

Sandy Hurt, the good friend who accompanied me to New Orleans and helped to make that research trip both productive and enjoyable.

The staff of the **Williams Research Library** of New Orleans, where I found most of my material.

Father Earl F. Niehaus, author of *The Irish in New Orleans,* for cheerfully answering all my questions.

Thanks also to:

Betty Whitaker, Mary Golichowski and my nephew **Paul Bennett,** all of whom read my manuscript and spurred me on, and to my fellow members of the **AAUW Creative Writers.**

Finally, thanks to:

Simon

My son, **Andy Gaus,** a writer himself , who has provided sharp editorial assistance along with unfailing support, and

Katherine Harman Harding, who took time from her numerous art projects to create the illustrations for this book. Both of them have been essential to this project.

I

A New World

"Glory be to God—This is America!" exclaimed twelve-year-old Simon O'Shea as he stepped out of the Customs House onto the levee in New Orleans. The day was Tuesday, May 9th, 1849.

The O'Sheas were a bedraggled group, two parents and four children, reeling on the first dry land they had encountered since leaving famine-stricken Ireland. They could have posed as a typical immigrant family—the father, Thomas, wearing a tall Irish hat; the mother, Martha, with a shawl wrapped over her head and shoulders and a small boy, five-year-old Kevin, clinging tightly to her hand. The three older children, Simon, ten-year-old Maggie and eight-year-old John, were all dressed in sturdy, brown, travel-weary clothes, much too warm for the bright, hot afternoon. A motley collection of sacks surrounded them.

They didn't feel like types, however; each of them felt like an adventurer in an extraordinary place. Maggie jumped up and down with excitement, her pigtails bobbing while John stood stock still, his eyes wide with wonder. Simon was filled with almost unbearable excitement. This was the land in which he would grow to manhood and where he expected to do great things. He burst out again, "Da, did you know it would be like this?"

*   *   *

They were standing on the brink of a whirlpool of activity—their eyes, their ears and even their noses assaulted by strangeness. None of them had ever seen people with different colors of skin. Now, they were gazing at a moving throng which contained more black faces than white and so many colors in between. Black women wearing high turbans of red and purple and orange walked by in stately fashion. Street vendors wound their way through the crowd calling and singing in a strange language. A peculiar smell of coffee, fish and exotic spices heightened the sense of foreignness.

*   *   *

"Peace, lad, give us a chance. Of course, I didn't know just what it would be like, but I knew we were coming to a New World and that it would be different from the old one; so did you. We have a lot to learn, but we'll have time to do it."

Martha said wonderingly, "Thomas, it's like the tower of Babel. We'll have to find our courage for sure and ask the good Lord to please make someone understand us."

"I'm sure He will, wife. Many of our countrymen have come this way before us. They managed and so will we. Right now, we have to find a barrow for our luggage."

"Over there, Da. I see a man with barrows!" Maggie grabbed her father's hand and pointed to a man on the edge

· 2 ·

of the crowd who was calling and gesticulating toward his wares.

"Good for you, Miss Sharp Eyes. Since you spotted the man and you have a dreadful hard time standing still you can come with me. The rest of you stay right here with your mother. Watch the luggage and, by all that's holy, stay together. I'll not be searching for any wandering body in all this confusion. Once we're loaded we'll start for the O'Malleys."

*   *   *

Oh, yes, the O'Malleys, thought Simon—they had been such good friends and good neighbors in Dublin. Both families experienced a hard wrench when they left Ireland four long years ago. After a while, Thomas O'Shea began to receive letters from Daniel O'Malley, saying that he had found a demand for skills in New Orleans, that he had been able to establish himself as a cabinet maker and was able to take good care of his family. He felt sure that a skilled blacksmith like Thomas could do equally well, and he urged Thomas to bring his family to New Orleans when he finally made the decision to emigrate. He also wrote, "When you come, you will, of course, come first to us."

What a great thing it would be to see them again! Still, Simon was a little apprehensive. Patrick O'Malley had played kick-the-can and other children's games with him in former days, but he was an older boy, tall and good looking even at ten—fourteen now and apprenticed to his father. Might he barely remember Simon and think him too young and too small to be his friend? His small stature plagued Simon. He prayed over it fervently. He didn't ask to be a great tall man. He just wanted to reach a good middle height like his father, Thomas, but he yearned to reach it soon. He thought if he had five or six more inches he wouldn't be worrying about Patrick. Well, he'd just have to bide his time and not appear too anxious.

Maggie was luckier. She and Brigid O'Malley were the same age and had been inseparable friends as well as neighbors. Both of them had wept desperately over having to part. Simon had no doubt that they would easily pick up at ten where they had so painfully left off at six.

As for John O'Shea and Michael O'Malley, they were only four when an ocean came between them, but John had such a calm, easy disposition he could fit in anywhere.

O'Malley was just a name to Kevin, who was only a baby when they left, and Maureen, the youngest O'Malley, hadn't even been born yet!

A yank on his jacket interrupted Simon's reverie. Kevin was hopping up and down, "Here they come, they've got a barrow."

So they did. Simon hove to and threw on sacks with a will. It felt good to do something.

*　　　　　　　*　　　　　　　*

"All right, everybody, pay attention," said Thomas. "These are your marching orders. We are going to make our way through all this confusion and head west first on Market Street and then on Tchoupitoulas. I know it's a funny name, but it's what we are looking for. I have directions to the

O'Malleys' so I will lead the way with your mother and Kevin behind me. Maggie and John are to follow and Simon can bring up the rear with the barrow. Once we get through the crowd, we can take turns pushing, but for now I just want to get us all safely through and on our way. Stay together, but if by any chance we get separated, remember the names of the streets and that we're heading toward the sun!"

The O'Sheas fell into position and plunged forward toward their new life. Simon fell slightly behind because he had to maneuver his cargo around vendors. What he found puzzling was that those he saw were almost all "people of color" going about their business with confidence. They certainly didn't appear to be slaves. If they were, then slavery was not such a bad thing after all.

A woman balancing a huge tray on her head stopped right in front of him to sell some kind of a small pie. Simon pulled up suddenly so as not to run into her. She said something unintelligible to her customer, took his money and handed over whatever the foodstuff was. She then continued weaving her way along, totally unconcerned. Simon couldn't help looking after her in wonderment at the ease with which she balanced her oversized burden. As a result, he barely managed to sidestep a man holding up a wrapped product and calling out its virtues. Simon had no trouble understanding that message. The smell of fish overcomes any language barrier.

Just as he caught up with his family, his attention turned to gangs of men who were working at full speed loading a steamboat. One group was heaving huge sacks and bales from the dock and throwing them to others on board. All of them were shouting at the top of their lungs. Simon had no trouble understanding them either. Swearing is swearing in any language.

WOMAN SELLING FOODSTUFFS FROM HER HAT

No sooner had he taken note of them than Simon saw a totally different sight: three white men roughly shoving five or six black men and a boy about his own age. The boy was manacled to one of the white men. All of them were headed toward the steamboat and an obviously forced boarding. Nobody in the crowd paid the slightest attention.

Suddenly, the boy turned and looked right at Simon. Desolation poured from his whole being. Simon felt it like a blow. Somehow, he knew he was looking at a boy who never expected to see his family again. This was slavery, and it was horrifying.

Simon

SLAVE AND FREE

II

Finding the Way

They still had to push through a lot of pedestrians, but the frenzied activity and the clamor that went with it began to diminish. Thomas took over the barrow and led the way. In a couple of blocks when they found themselves on Tchoupitoulas, they were able to look around more and take note of their surroundings. Huge trees with moss hanging down from them like giant beards dominated the scene. Ireland had nothing like that! Martha exclaimed about the flowers,

"Just look, all those beautiful vines with purple flowers and the lovely pink ones in the yards. What do you suppose they are?"

"I'm sure Agnes will be able to tell you, Thomas replied. "I can't look at anything but the balconies with all their iron work, and right in front of us is an iron gate with an elaborate design such as I have never seen. Daniel told me New Orleans is a great place for blacksmiths."

"Could you make railings and gates like that, Da?" asked Maggie.

Simon

WROUGHT IRON RAILINGS

"I should have the craft to do it, lass, if I had some practice. It's certainly not what I'm going to try to do first, but it looks mighty interesting."

On they walked, not talking much, unable to absorb all they saw. They felt like the greenhorns they were. After they had passed several groups jabbering away in French, John asked plaintively, "Da, will the O'Malleys still speak English?"

Thomas gave a great shout, "Indeed and indeed and they will, Boyo. Have no fear. We'll be seeing them soon." Everybody laughed and the whole family picked up their pace. Simon was again pushing the barrow when, at last, they reached St. Thomas Street, encountered two men talking on the corner and heard the welcome sound of Irish brogue "God be praised, we're going to be all right now," Thomas said as he approached the men.

"Excuse me, I'm Thomas O'Shea, just arrived from Dublin. Could either of you gentlemen be after telling me whether I'm headed right for Fulton Street? I'm looking for Daniel O'Malley."

"Indeed we could, lad. I'm Tim Flannery and this is John O'Connor. We both know Daniel, and we've been hearing about Daniel's great friends, the O'Sheas and all their good children for weeks now. Welcome to New Orleans. Just keep going. You'll find yourselves in Lafayette in a few minutes."

"What's Lafayette?" interrupted ever-inquisitive Maggie. "Aren't we staying in New Orleans?"

"It's a separate town, lass, even though you only have to cross Felicity Street to get into it. After that you'll have six more blocks to Fulton Street. Just turn on to it and you'll find the O'Malleys in the third house on the right. There'll be a grand excitement."

III

Reunion with Old Friends

The rest of the family got ahead of Simon as he maneuvered the clumsy vehicle around the corner. Suddenly a little girl sitting on the stoop of a house down the street leapt to her feet and ran toward them shouting, "Maggie!"

Maggie rushed forward with an answering cry of "Brigid!" and, in only seconds, the two girls were hugging and laughing and crying. The commotion brought Agnes O'Malley out the door and she too began exclaiming,

"Thomas, Martha. By all the saints, you're the most welcome sight that ever came down this street. Brigid, run down to the shop and tell your Da and Patrick the O'Sheas are here and, yes, you can take Maggie with you. I know you won't let her get lost. Come in, dear friends, rest a little and take some nourishment."

Gratefully, the travelers stepped into a spacious, hospitable room. Light from the late afternoon sun streamed across a massive table in the center of the room with chairs at either end and benches along the sides. The O'Sheas' attention, however, was drawn first to the corner where enticing smells came from a pot simmering on the stove. They not only drank in the aroma, they all gasped at the sight of a full bin of potatoes. Agnes laughed:

"It's going to be a grand treat to feed you, for sure. First, if you go straight on through you'll find the privy in the backyard. Then, come in the bedroom and wash the dust of the journey off your hands. There's water in the pitcher and soap in the dish. I'll put bread and milk out for you now. For supper, I need only add some of those potatoes to the stew pot. You are not going to go hungry in New Orleans."

The travelers did as they were told, the parents first, then the children. A sense of ease lapped over Simon as he felt the cool water on his hands—how wonderful to be in this house and in this room!

The washstand they were using stood at the foot of a large bed with a trundle underneath. Across the room were a clothes press and a crib. A couple of chairs completed the furnishings—comfort, space, cleanliness. What a contrast to the six weeks on shipboard!

*   *   *

The O'Sheas and their fellow passengers had been crowded together with only meager opportunities for washing. Almost immediately they were breathing fetid air. When stormy weather began to rock the ship creating an epidemic of seasickness, the stench became almost unbearable. Seamen swabbed the quarters frequently, but with little effect.

Fortunately, the last ten days of the voyage had been sunny with only light winds. Passengers were allowed out on deck in small groups and given opportunities to wash both themselves and their clothing. They had managed to arrive in New Orleans looking presentable. Still, this clean, orderly environment was overwhelming. It left them all wide-eyed and temporarily speechless.

The silence ended with exclamations as they returned to the main room and saw the loaf of bread, the tub of butter and the pitcher of milk on the table.

"Jesus, Mary and Joseph, look at that fresh-baked bread and all that milk," burst out of John.

"Don't look at it, eat and drink," replied Agnes, "but you don't need to hurry; you'll be having supper soon."

They did as they were told, remembering to give a quick prayer of thanks and trying not to wolf their food. Simon had barely taken the edge off his hunger when he heard rushing footsteps and a great shout from Daniel O'Malley,

"Thomas and Martha, stay right where you are and rest your weariness. Just let me drink in the sight of your whole grand family sitting around my table. We have been waiting so eagerly for this moment, haven't we, Patrick?"

"That we have." Patrick greeted Mr. and Mrs. O'Shea then walked quickly around to Simon and clapped him on the shoulder:

"It's right glad I am to see you, lad. I hope you haven't forgotten me, because I'm eager to show you New Orleans."

"No chance, Patrick. I was afraid you might be too grand to bother yourself with me now that you're a cabinet maker's apprentice. Show me around as much as you like."

*   *   *

Soon, the commotion died down as Brigid and Maggie, still not willing to be separated, brought twelve steaming bowls of stew to the table. Daniel O'Malley asked God's blessing on the food and offered a brief thanksgiving for friends reunited. After which, all those friends devoted themselves single-mindedly to the most satisfying meal of their lives.

When the travelers sighed with repletion, Agnes took charge:

"Before we clean up and start on all the things we have to talk about, let's settle where everybody is to sleep. We have two bedrooms. Daniel and I and Maureen sleep in the room where you washed your hands. I thought we'd put the girls in the trundle bed there. The other bedroom is similarly furnished, but without a crib. Thomas and Martha get the big bed, of course. The three younger boys can snuggle together in the trundle.

"That leaves pallets for Patrick and Simon—the only question is where do they want to put those pallets. I doubt they'll choose to be crowded in with everybody else. They could doss down in this room or, on a nice night like this, they could choose the back yard—provided they shroud themselves in mosquito netting, of which we have plenty."

Simon held his breath and looked at Patrick—what would he want? The answer came quickly,

"Well, Simon, what say you? Shall we brave the great outdoors?"

"Oh, yes, if it's all right with you."

"Good, if you're going to live in New Orleans you'll have to learn to protect yourself from mosquitoes, and you might as well start now."

At that moment, Simon would have followed Patrick anywhere.

Agnes stepped first into the backyard and quickly filled a pan with water from the cistern. She then carried a sleepy Maureen to her crib while the two girls washed, dried and put away the bowls and spoons. Everyone began making sleeping arrangements.

Brigid and Maggie pulled out the trundle bed, saw that it had a sheet, a light blanket and a pillow and then sat down on it, prepared to entertain the baby until she fell asleep. On the other side of the house John, Michael and Kevin pulled out their trundle bed, saw that it too was ready for sleeping. They bounced up and down on it, found it to their satisfaction, and without discussion elected to stay there, talking and giggling until sleep overtook them.

Meanwhile, Patrick led Simon out to the back yard to set up their sleeping arrangements while the last of the daylight remained. The yard was not large, but it held more than a privy and a cistern. A tall tree, dripping with moss like so many they had noticed on their journey, extended its branches from one corner to provide welcome shade for much of the area. Simon saw a neat green vegetable garden in the sunnier section, but Patrick didn't give him time to see what all was growing in it. He took Simon immediately to a shed in the other corner saying, "We have to move fast to out-wit the mosquitoes."

Together, the boys pulled out a small tent, two pallets and a big roll of what had to be mosquito netting. Patrick quickly set up the tent, draped a double layer of mosquito netting over it and Simon slid the two pallets inside.

Slapping themselves against the eager enemy the two boys jumped back into the house, where they joined the adults around the table.

*   *   *

Daniel began the evening's talk: "Thomas, we know there's the terrible starvation all over our poor Ireland, but tell us what's happened to all the old neighbors."

"They are almost all gone—the Murphys and the Dohertys sailed to New York in 1847 and the Carmodys to Boston the following year. I think they are getting along all right, but I haven't heard recently. I was the last holdout on our block except for poor Mrs. Sweeney, who has no way to escape except to Heaven, God bless her.

"I kept hoping for better things—for the famine to end and the taxation and penal laws to be lifted. I took heart from the protests raised in both England and France. Voices were raised in Parliament calling for relief for the poor suffering Irish, but it all came to nothing. When last year's uprising failed so miserably, I knew we had to leave."

"All that misery hardly bears thinking on, Thomas, but it will be better here. I think I'm after knowing where you can find work. There is a blacksmith's shop less than a mile away. The owner is a German, Hans Grossmann. He has been here ten years. His partner died last winter and he now has more work than he can keep up with. I've known him a long time. He's a master smith, and he's mighty particular. You should be just what he is looking for. He knows you are coming. I'm sure he'll give you a chance."

"That's grand news indeed. I've already seen enough of New Orleans to learn that it's a great place for iron working. I'll go tomorrow as fast as my legs will carry me. Shall I take Simon with me? He wants to be apprenticed as soon as it's possible."

"Well, I doubt that it's possible just yet. You're twelve aren't you Simon? When will you be thirteen?"

"In September."

Simon could barely breathe. Was he going to be able to start preparing for a man's work or was he going to have to hang around for months with the women and the younger children? He wished more than ever that he were bigger. The easy tone of Daniel's answer brought relief:

"That's not so long. The usual age for apprenticeship here, Thomas, is fourteen just as it is in Ireland, but it's not a strict rule. I got Patrick started at thirteen, and he was able to make himself useful around the shop before he was apprenticed. I have an idea that Simon has some advantages neither of you may realize. Do you write a legible hand, Simon?"

"Yes, sir, I think so. I've had no complaints." *What did handwriting have to do with blacksmithing?*

"That's good. I also seem to remember that even as a little fellow you were a dab at sums. Isn't that right?"

"I guess so. I've always liked figuring."

Simon's astonishment and puzzlement were so apparent that Daniel laughed as he explained: "A busy workman, especially a blacksmith, often has trouble keeping up with his accounts. People come in with broken tools, wagons to be mended, horses to be shod. Everyone wants his attention at once. If the smith has a lad around who can write down who owes how much for what work or who is leaving work to be done later, it makes his life much easier."

Once that grand idea had been put forward, it was decided unanimously that both Thomas and Simon should offer their services to Herr Grossmann in the morning and that now it was time for bed.

Patrick said, "All right, Simon, we're going to make a quick dive onto our pallets. I'm sure you're going to do well in New Orleans, but it's not Paradise. We have mosquitoes."

"And slavery."

"Yes, but we don't have slavery here in Lafayette, and we do have mosquitoes, so let's try to avoid them as much as we can."

IV

Herr Grossmann

Simon woke at daybreak, bewildered at first to find himself in a tent with a stranger sleeping beside him. He quickly realized, however, that Patrick was no stranger and that he, Simon O'Shea, was lying beside a friend and facing one of the crucial days of his life. He was glad to have a few private moments to contemplate it. He had never known any Germans and the smith sounded formidable. *Could an aspiring twelve-year-old possibly pass muster with Herr Grossmann?*

Well, Daniel O'Malley seemed to think he could, and everything had gone well so far. His fears about Patrick had certainly proved groundless.

Just then, as though he had been called, Patrick woke up, stretched and said, "Top of the morning, Simon. We'd best get moving. This is a big day."

The boys scrambled into their clothes, splashed water from the cistern on their faces to help wake themselves up and went into the house. There they found their fathers already at table. Agnes greeted them with, "Sit down, laddies. Workingmen get served first. I want you fed and on your way. Once you're gone we have a lot to do here too."

With that, she placed bread and butter and milk in front of them.

Being called a workingman gave Simon a small warm spurt of confidence.

Daniel said a quick grace and they ate quickly as they had been told. When they had finished, Agnes gave them each a wrapped package of bread and cheese for their lunch. They were on their way!

They began by retracing part of the route from yesterday. They didn't talk much, but, as they reached Daniel's workshop, Patrick told his friend, "You'll get along fine with Herr Grossmann. Just don't expect a German to tell you what a grand fellow you are."

*　　　*　　　*

Then they were on their own with final instructions from Daniel: "Keep on for three more blocks, turn right for a block then left, and you'll see the smithy. God be with you."

Simon's heart pounded as they turned the final corner. They spotted the smithy instantly. The building stood well back from the street with a couple of trees providing shade for the cinder-covered yard in front. The yard held a couple of wagons and some other implements that looked as though they were waiting to be repaired. A stack of old iron leaned against the building, and a horse, apparently ready to be shod, stood tied at the hitching rail. Now that they had come so close, the man and boy approached slowly.

They saw the smith come out of the shop, untie the horse and lead him in without haste. From the yard, they watched as he picked up the left hind foot, caught it between his aproned knees and laid a shoe on it. The shoe was too wide at the heel and Herr Grossmann let the horse's foot go back to the floor, caught the shoe in his tongs and shoved it in among the coals in his forge. He cranked the bellows and made small flames spike up out of the coals. As he turned the handle he looked at the light of the open doorway, but didn't really see Thomas and Simon as the light shone in his eyes.

They saw him though, a medium-sized man with powerful shoulders and a no-nonsense air about him. His hair was grizzled, and his face and arms were shining with sweat. Presently, he drew the glowing shoe out of the coals, laid it on the horn of the anvil and turned in the heel. He then plunged the shoe into a tub of water from which it drew a brief shriek of steam.

Thomas whispered to Simon, "This is a good place. I already like the way the man works." In a minute, the smith took the cooled shoe from the tub and, picking up the horse's foot and straddling it again quickly nailed the shoe on. The owner paid him and led his horse out.

By this time Herr Grossmann had noticed his visitors and said brusquely, "I'll take care of you when I'm free. Are you O'Malley's friend?" Thomas nodded his assent.

"Come in and look around. I'll talk to you just as soon as I have taken care of these men who are waiting for me."

They stepped in. Thomas liked the look of the shop as much as he liked the work of its master. The workspace was as tidy as any blacksmith could make it, every surface swept and every tool in its place. Workbenches circled three walls. The forge and two anvils, one large and one small, stood in front near the open door. Simon liked the way the shop looked too, but mostly he felt relief at how easy and confident his father seemed in this environment. He would try to act the same way.

In a short time, the smith took care of his two customers, then turned and said, "All right, now...."

*　　　*　　　*

"As you guessed, I'm Daniel O'Malley's friend, Thomas O'Shea, a blacksmith from Dublin, sore in need of a job and eager to be of help in this grand shop of yours. This is my son Simon, who hopes to be apprenticed soon."

Herr Grossmann looked the applicants over, acknowledged the introduction with a nod, and sat down on the bench behind him, motioning them to do likewise:

"I understand you've been a carriage maker. How long is it since you have shod a horse or a mule?"

"It has been a while, but I've done it often enough in my day. That is not a skill that a man forgets. I served my seven years of apprenticeship and worked as a general smith for several years before I turned to making carriages. I should be able to help you with anything that comes in unless it would be orders for fancy gates and railings such as I never saw until yesterday. Is that part of your trade?"

"I do a little of it, but not much. Lafayette has been settled mostly by German and, more recently, Irish immigrants. We've not been accustomed to decorating our houses with iron. Still, wrought iron is a feature of all the handsome homes in New Orleans. As people around here begin to prosper, they want to use it too. If you stay, you'll probably want to try your hand.

"Work's been piling up since my partner died, Thomas. Just shoeing the horses and mules and keeping all the wagons in repair seems to eat up most of my time. I have an order on hand for andirons and decorative fireplace tools along with a large assortment of interior and exterior hinges for a house that's half built. I'm turning away all other such jobs until I get that one done.

"I do need help, but I'll need to see your work and how we shake down together before I consider an agreement. Put on that apron now. We'll see if you can make yourself useful. I'll pay you whatever seems reasonable. Does that suit you?"

"Indeed it does."

As Simon was beginning to wonder whether either of them remembered he was there, Herr Grossmann turned a penetrating gaze in his direction, while still addressing his father:

"The lad looks all too young for apprenticeship."

"Yes," replied Thomas easily. "We know he is not quite ready to be apprenticed. He is only twelve and he doesn't have his size yet, but he is

right handy and he is eager to learn. He hopes to start apprenticeship when he is thirteen, which will be in September.

"The usual beginning age for apprenticeship in Ireland is fourteen just as it is here, but Simon is already well schooled. He writes a neat hand and he is good at figures. While he is waiting to get a little older and a little bigger, he'd like to be observing the work in the shop, making himself useful however he can, perhaps helping with your book work if you would let him."

Simon could scarcely breathe. He could tell nothing from looking at Herr Grossmann except that he was deliberating. Patrick had warned— don't expect a German to act like an Irishman. Finally, the verdict came.

"I see no reason he shouldn't come if he can manage to stay out of the way and not ask too many questions. I don't really need a clerk, but it might be useful. We can see how it works out. Are we all agreed?"

"Oh, yes, sir. Thank you sir."

Just then four or five customers came into the smithy at once. The smith went forward to meet them, saying "Come, Thomas," and to Simon brusquely, "Just stay out of the way."

Simon did as he was told, feeling fairly unimportant, but as he watched the two men confer with the customers and with each other, he remembered Patrick's *Don't expect him to tell you what a grand lad you are.*

∗   ∗   ∗

Rebuffed or not, he sat quietly. It dawned on him that he was extremely tired, and gradually he relaxed. Images of the last two days ran through his mind: being herded through the Custom House with a tag around his neck as though he were a parcel, stepping out on the levee for his first full view of the port of New Orleans, inhaling all its peculiar smells, listening to the foreign sounds, dodging the vendors, and being shocked by the misery of the slave boy. When he remembered arriving at the O'Malleys', and all that had happened there, a sense of ease overcame him.

He caught himself about to fall off the bench. *Had he been asleep for long? Oh, what a disaster it would be to fall and have to be picked up like a baby!*

He looked up cautiously to see whether he had been observed, but saw no one. Voices were audible from the yard, however, so after stretching to get rid of his stiffness, Simon walked to the doorway.

Two men, holding their horses by the reins, stood by the wagons, talking to the smiths. Apparently, both wagons had been repaired. *He must have slept a long time! What should he do?*

He remembered his instructions and just watched as the men concluded their business, hitched the horses to the wagons and drove away.

Simon tried not to quiver as his father and Herr Grossmann turned toward him. They both looked him over. What would they say? Herr Grossmann spoke first, "Well, Simon, were your dreams happy?"

"No, sir. I didn't dream at all. I didn't mean to go to sleep on the job. I'm sorry, sir."

The hitherto gruff smith actually laughed, "You weren't sleeping on the job, Simon. You don't *have* a job. Come back rested in the morning. We'll see how things go."

V

Reminiscing with the O'Malleys

Father and son retraced their footsteps to the O'Malleys'. Maggie and Brigid were in front of the house just as Brigid had been the day before. It already felt almost like coming home. Maggie was jumping with news and questions: "Do you have a job, Da? Did you like Herr Grossmann? Is he going to let Simon keep coming? Wait till you hear all the things we did today."

Martha, who was just coming out the door, expostulated, "Slow down, lass. Let the rest of us welcome your Da and then give him a chance to answer. I want to know those things too. We all do." By this time the whole household had gathered excitedly, except for Daniel and Patrick, who were still at work.

"Well," said Thomas, "I don't exactly have a job, but my prospects look good. I'm to work for Herr Grossmann for a couple of weeks to give him time to see how able a smith I am and how well we work together.

"So far, we are getting along fine."

"Yes, I think he is a man I would be glad to work for. He doesn't say much, but I admire the work he does and the way he keeps his shop. Simon's situation is much the same as mine. He can keep coming for a while, and he'll probably get a chance to show he can be useful. It has been a good day. Wouldn't you say so, son?"

"Oh, yes," agreed Simon with relief. *Apparently his Da wasn't going to tell about his sleeping most of the afternoon.*

Martha's face shone with pleasure, but she said only, "That's grand news. Now we'd best let Maggie tell about our day before she bursts."

*   *   *

"We've done so many things. We got all our stuff unpacked, and we went to market! You'd never believe all the food they have—a lot of things I never saw before, much less tasted. It's not a bit like poor Ireland.

"Mrs. O'Malley is already teaching Ma and me to cook New Orleans food. You'll be surprised by your supper and some other things too!"

"Well, may Simon and I come in and wash off some of the day's dust before we start getting all those surprises?"

Everybody laughed and moved out of the way. Simon found as much pleasure in washing up as he had the day before, but it was different. Yesterday, his satisfaction had come from being in a clean, peaceful, uncluttered space. Today, it came from the sense of fellowship with his father—two men sharing a basin of water after a long, satisfying day at work (never mind that Simon hadn't actually done any work, he'd been sort of accepted by the smith, and he was going back tomorrow).

Daniel and Patrick came in shortly, equally eager to know how the day had gone. When Daniel, who knew Hans Grossmann fairly well, heard Thomas's report, he said at once, "That's a wonderful lot for a close-mouthed German to say. If you still do know how to shoe a horse, you shouldn't have any worries. No doubt, Simon will prove himself too."

*   *   *

Once Daniel and Patrick had had a chance to wash off the dust of their day's work, Agnes called them all to the table, which was set with plates and mugs. She placed a large tureen in front of Daniel's place. Maggie was proudly pouring milk into the mugs from a colorful blue and orange pitcher—the O'Shea pitcher brought all the way across the ocean.

Simon was amazed by how glad he was at the sight of it. He remembered his parents talking about what one household object they should take to remind them of the life they were leaving. Thomas said to Martha, "It's your choice, wife."

Simon had thought then that it didn't matter at all, but now seeing the familiar pitcher in this new place, he found it remarkably handsome and thought his mother had made the perfect decision. He didn't want to forget Ireland!

THE O'SHEA PITCHER

After asking the blessing, Daniel filled their plates from the tureen.

Agnes said, "You're going to have something you have never had before. I am hoping you'll manage to eat it because it's a New Orleans standby." She then gave the newcomers their first taste of crayfish. They all ate with gusto and Thomas declared:

"Agnes, this dish is a great credit to the markets of New Orleans and to your hand at the stove. Please go on teaching my wife and daughter!"

*   *   *

Once they had all settled down, Patrick remarked, "Simon, don't you think it's surprising that we are both getting started ahead of ourselves over here because of going to that hateful school, or didn't you mind beginning every morning with:

I thank the Goodness and the Grace
That on my birth have smiled,
And made me in these Christian days,
A happy English child?

"I certainly despised reciting that verse, although it was less awful after I learned about keeping my fingers crossed. The last two years I had a teacher who didn't make us say it, and I liked school a good deal better. Still, I always thought it would have been much more exciting to go to hedge schools like our parents did."

John interrupted here, "Why were hedge schools exciting, Da?"

"Because the penal laws forbade any schooling of Catholic children. Believe me, lawbreaking is exciting as long as you don't get caught. We met in secret places, always keeping a sharp watch for 'the enemy.' We felt clever and oh, so brave, and we learned all we could. Actually, the only risk was to our teachers, especially if they were priests.

"We all knew about Tim Kelly's cousin, Father Joe, arrested in front of a class of students and carted away. His family didn't know whether he was alive or dead. They thought he was in jail, but they hoped he had escaped. They didn't dare inquire."

"Why did the hedge schools stop?"

"Because the English finally established schools that all Irish children, even you, could go to. They aren't exciting, and they try to make Brits and Protestants out of you, but they reach a lot more children. Since they meet regularly and provide books, they can teach reading, writing and figuring much better than our more exciting schools could.

"We didn't have books so we could only learn by listening, but our teachers knew history, poetry and religion and they loved the Irish language. We are all going to be Americans now, but we who had the benefit of hedge schools will try to pass on some of your Irish heritage—not tonight though. It's time to rest for another day."

VI

Brambles on the Path

When the two older boys had dodged the mosquitoes as best they could and were again lying side by side in the tent, Patrick said, "It is so good to have you here, Simon. Lots of Irish folk are settled in Lafayette, but this is the first time in four years that I've talked to anybody who lived on Duke Street and shared our life in Dublin. It was fun tonight to talk about that school we went to and to hear our parents tell about their hedge schools.

"I'm right eager to show you New Orleans. Da says I can have Saturday off so we can go into town together. I do so want you to like it here."

"Of course, I like it. You have all been wonderful. Even Herr Grossmann is better than I expected. Da didn't tell anybody, but after we all had our talk, a lot of customers came in the shop. Herr Grossmann put Da right to work and ordered me sharply to 'just keep out of the way.' I sat down and watched a little while, but it was hot and I was tired. Next thing I knew I caught myself almost falling off the bench. I guess I had slept the afternoon away. I was really scared of what Herr Grossmann would say. He said I hadn't slept on the job because I didn't have a job, but he laughed when he said it.

"The only thing I don't like about New Orleans is slavery. Right after we got off the boat I saw a slave boy, handcuffed to a white man, being shoved toward a steamboat. The boy turned around and looked right at me. He looked so desperate. I haven't been able to get him out of my mind."

"Simon, don't fret. There is nothing you could have done for that boy anymore than you could have fed the starving children in Ireland. You just got off the boat! You're not even a citizen and you're only twelve. It's daft to worry about things you can't help.

"None of us *likes* slavery, but there are no slave-holders in Lafayette, and I just tell myself that the slaves are at least not starving. New Orleans has more free people of color than any other Southern city."

"Why is that?"

"It's because New Orleans used to be French, and the French had a different approach to slavery than the Americans. I'll tell you more about that when I get to show you around. Now it is time for sleep. Stop worrying. Good night to you, Simon."

Patrick fell asleep at once, but Simon found himself struggling with a hard core of resistance. *Starving children in Ireland didn't make slavery all right in America.* Patrick hadn't really said they did. He just said he wasn't worrying about it, and Simon shouldn't either. Still, it was thoroughly unsatisfying.

Simon couldn't *help* worrying. He couldn't find any good way to argue with Patrick, but he didn't like being called daft. He lay awake a long time fussing over this first break in his admiration for his friend. He thought about what he had learned from his Da about the American Revolution and Patrick Henry's cry of "Give me liberty or give me death!"

Would Da say the same things about slavery that Patrick said? Simon was afraid to find out. Finally, he gave it up and slept briefly.

VII

Back to the Smithy

When he awoke next morning, he saw Patrick already on his feet and pulling on his clothes. He scrambled to catch up, and the two boys joined their fathers for a quick breakfast before starting to work. It hardly seemed possible to Simon that they had been in New Orleans for only two days. Yesterday, they only hoped they were going to find work. Today they were starting off for a job—even if it was only on approval. Simon hoped fervently that his Da really did remember how to shoe a horse.

When they turned the final corner, he realized he was about to find out. Six horses and their owners were waiting in front of the smithy, and as he looked, Herr Grossmann opened the doors and came out.

"You're just in time. Gentlemen, this is Thomas, my new assistant. As soon as he puts his apron on, he will shoe your horses for you. He tells me he has had a lot of experience."

Simon quivered. Herr Grossmann hadn't even spoken to him and his Da had been presented with a test. No fooling around. This was it. *Please, God, let it go well.*

*   *   *

Thomas with his blacksmith's apron in place stepped up to the first horse, led him into the smithy without the slightest sign of strain, picked up the left hind foot, straddled it just as Herr Grossmann had the day before and proceeded to fit the shoe. He acted as if he had been doing it every day of his life. Herr Grossmann barked out, "Simon."

"Yes, sir."

"Come here and look at my books," and—to the customer, "The lad is going to try his hand at bookkeeping."

"Write down on this line: 1 horseshoe 50 cents. Then mark it paid in the next column. The money goes in this box here. I take care of that. I'll show you later what you do when work is left to be picked up."

One of the men waiting said: "Is that Daniel O'Malley's friend shoeing the horse?"

"Yes, he's my acting assistant. I'm trying him out."

"He looks right at home already. I'll have a word with him once he's finished nailing on that shoe. I guess he's done now—

"Thomas, give us your hand. I'm Michael Kelly, friend to your friend, O'Malley. Welcome to Lafayette and to New Orleans. Will we be seeing you on Sunday at St. Pat's?"

"God willing, we'll be there. I hear it's a grand, fine church."

"Well, it's not quite finished and there have been troubles along the way, but it's mighty handsome already, and Father Mullon is a treat to hear. Is that your lad helping with the books?"

"Indeed, it is. Simon, come meet Mr. Kelly; he's a friend of the O'Malleys."

"Well, Simon, are you after becoming a blacksmith like your Da?"

"Yes, sir, as soon as I'm allowed to be old enough."

"Old enough or not, you're in a grand shop for learning the trade. Let's hope you don't have to wait too long."

"Thank you, sir."

Three more men came in just as Simon returned to his post. Saying,

"Just watch," Herr Grossmann stepped forward to take care of them. "Just watch" sounded a lot friendlier than "keep out of the way" had the day before. Mr. Kelly had been encouraging too. Simon began to feel almost at ease.

The shop continued busy. Men came in with tools to be mended, wagons to be repaired and, something that intrigued Simon, wooden wheels to be fitted with iron tires. Herr Grossmann said he couldn't do those right away, but would get to them as soon as possible on Friday.

Most of the customers were good humored, although a couple came in cursing their equipment for breaking down, and obviously begrudging the money for repairs. Simon noted with interest that Herr Grossmann remained calm and implacable in the face of these surly characters and made sure they paid before he released their equipment. He then ordered his new clerk to enter the transactions.

Right after that a distraught but polite young man came in with two pieces of broken metal.

"Oh, Herr Grossmann, I loaded my wagon this morning, but barely got started when this singletree broke in half. I can't so much as turn a wheel until it's fixed. Can you possibly do it quickly?"

"You're in luck, John. I've been watching a possible new assistant—to see how he goes about shoeing a horse. He doesn't need my watching. I can take care of your singletree right now."

"I can't pay until I get my wagon rolling and make my deliveries."

Saying, "It's all right. I know you're good for it," the smith quietly wrote the debt down himself in another part of the account book. Then said to Simon,

"Wagon repairs are as big a part of blacksmithing as horse-shoeing. Take a break now, lad, and have your lunch. Your fader can join you as soon as he finishes with that last horse. Busy days like this I just eat at the desk whenever I have a chance."

*   *   *

Simon obeyed with alacrity, repairing to the bench in the corner where they had all eaten the day before. It felt good to sit down. The bread, cheese and fruit all tasted wonderful. While he was eating, he picked up the *Daily Picayune,* which was folded to a page of advertisements. First to catch his eye was:

Valuable English Books
On view at 70 Chartres street, prior to sale by public auction.

The undersigned has received per Brutus from London, a consignment of 8,000 volumes of VALUABLE BOOKS, from the eminent publishing house of Henry J. Bohn. These comprise many of the best editions of Standard Works in Classics, History, Travels, Philosophy and the Fine Arts, including Heraldry and Illuminated Books....

Simon wasn't sure just what all those things were, heraldry, for instance, but he began to dream of a day when he could go to a sale like this with money in his pocket and find out what was in those valuable books. Next he noticed:

DAGUERREOTYPE

SALOONS

The Daguerreotype Saloons

93 Camp street, Shiff's New Buildings,

Are now open for the reception of visitors who are respectfully invited to examine the very extensive Collection of Portraits.
These Saloons have been magnificently furnished and every attention will be bestowed to give satisfaction to patrons....

Simon didn't have a great craving to have a photographic portrait of himself. He'd just as soon save that until he was taller, but he enjoyed the idea of the magnificent furnishings.

He was smiling as he turned the page over, but his mood changed abruptly. What he saw was:

SLAVES-SLAVES-SLAVES

NOTICE TO MERCHANTS, PLANTERS AND OTHERS

Having leased the Slave Depot, No.195 Gravior street, I take this method of informing my friends and the public generally that I am prepared to receive negroes on commission for sale. Having made large improvements to the premises, I am prepared to accommodate a large number. Persons having slaves for sale will find it to their advantage to give me a call. I have on hand a valuable lot of imported and acclimated Negroes for sale, consisting of field hands, house servants &c. Persons wishing to purchase will please give me a call.

C.F. HATCHER

Immediately under that were two smaller notices:

NEGROES-NEGROES

Just received and for sale at No. 7 Moreau street, Third Municipality, the largest and likeliest lot of Negroes ever imported by the Subscriber, consisting of Field Hands, House Servants and Mechanics. Will be receiving new lots regularly during the season.

WM. F. TAL-BOTT

And:

NEGROES FOR SALE—Four valuable Negroes, a man and three women for sale. Two of the women are good seam-stresses, and all of them likely and good house servants—fully guaranteed
PEGRAM & BRYAN, at 57 Gravier st.

*   *   *

Just then, Thomas joined him, and Simon burst out, "Da, look at this. They're selling Negroes like animals. Does it even *bother* you?"

Thomas leaned forward speaking urgently in a low voice, "Simon, *stop*! This is no place to discuss slavery, nor is that any way for you to speak to me. I'm flabbergasted that you would behave so. Don't *ever* do it again!

"*Of course*, selling people like animals bothers me. We can talk on the way home, if you can keep your voice down."

"Sorry, Da. I know it's not your fault. I'll try to behave."

*   *   *

The rest of the day went smoothly enough. Fewer customers came in, and Herr Grossmann took time to identify a few of the tools for Simon as he returned them to the rack: "This is the chisel I used to scarf the broken ends of that singletree I just welded. This is the hammer I used to pound them together after they were white hot. Different tools for different jobs. Each has its place. You'll learn."

When the time came to start for home, Simon felt considerable apprehension. *What would his Da say?* He walked along, silent and nervous, until he heard, "Well, Simon?" Then it all came pouring out:

          *   *   *

"Oh, Da, I've been fussing in my head about slavery ever since I saw a black boy at the dock manacled to a white man who was shoving him into a steamboat. I can't forget the way he turned and looked at me as though beseeching me to *do something*. I felt so helpless.

"I told Patrick about it last night and he told me that the slaves at least weren't starving, that New Orleans had more free people of color than any other Southern city, that I was only twelve years old and just off the boat and that I was daft to worry about things I couldn't help. Then he turned over and went to sleep.

"I couldn't find an answer to what he said and I couldn't sleep either. I got to thinking you'd probably tell me the same things—even though this is supposed to be the Land of the Free, and when I saw those slave advertisements, it just poured out. I'm sorry."

          *   *   *

Thomas sighed ruefully, "I do understand, Simon. I've been there myself. It's not just slavery that's bothering you. It's your new grand friend, Patrick, telling you to stop fretting about it. His advice was sensible. There's no way to argue with it. He just doesn't understand that you can't follow it. Don't hold that against Patrick. The good Lord made us all different, and nobody will ever try harder than Patrick has to be a true friend to you.

"Here we are. We'll talk about this some more another time."

VIII

Restful Interlude

Maggie was again stationed in the doorway ready to greet the two hot, sweaty workers from the smithy and give them the news of the day.

"We've been down at the river, scrubbing clothes. By all the saints, you look more than ready for your turn at soap and water. Then you can see what else has happened here—Maureen is walking."

"Ablutions before all else," agreed Thomas, and led the way to the washstand. Cool water finally soothed the itch of Simon's resentment and washed it away along with the sweat of the day. He went out happily to greet Daniel and Patrick and all the other members of the combined families.

After a supper of red beans and rice—*another New Orleans specialty, how many more would there be?*—they all settled down, adults on the chairs, children on the floor, while Maureen demonstrated her new wobbly skill with Brigid and Maggie acting as impresarios, "Come on, Maureen, show how you can walk!"

At first, Maureen took only two or three steps from one girl to the other, then ventured a little farther to other outstretched hands amid great applause. Finally, when Daniel held out both hands and called from across the room, "Come to your Da," she became more adventurous. Starting her journey over an obviously vast expanse, she promptly fell down. Everybody shouted out, "Oops-a-Baby, Get up, Keep going, girl," as Brigid rushed to put her back on her feet. Maureen clearly considered crying, then decided to laugh instead and staggered onward. This exact scene was repeated twice more. Each time she fell on her fifth step, but on the final try as her father bent even farther forward with arms outstretched, she took eight staggering steps and fell into his arms. Daniel swooped her into his lap and began to sing:

Bye O, baby O—look what Maureen can do
Bye O, mavourneen—Your Da's so proud of you
Bye O, baby O—It's walking you will go
Bye O, mavourneen—We all love you so.
He repeated this twice as his audience hummed an accompaniment, then finished with, Bye O,
baby O—Now it's time for bed
Sweet dreams, mavourneen—lay down your head.

As Agnes plucked the already sleeping baby from Daniel's lap and took her to her crib, Simon found himself struggling to keep his own eyes open. He suddenly remembered that he had hardly slept the night before. Deciding to give in, he said a quick good night,

"I'm going to have to head for the tent before somebody has to carry me too. Patrick, join me when you're ready, but you'll not find me awake. Sleep well everybody, I'll see you in the morning."

IX

Blacksmithing

Simon slept long and well. When he woke, noting that Patrick was up before him, he jumped into his clothes and joined the others at table for a quick breakfast of bread and milk, accompanied by taunting from Maggie,

"Here comes a new apprentice, so grand he chooses to sleep the hours away and go to work whenever he feels like it. Sure and Herr Grossmann is fortunate indeed to have found him."

"I am not keeping anybody waiting. I'm not an apprentice yet, and I'll be at work on time, even if I do have a sassy sister." With that, he set off for the smithy prepared for whatever the day might bring.

First, it brought a large number of German customers with horses needing to be shod. They were obviously a group of friends, talking jovially with each other and with Herr Grossmann in their native tongue, although they summoned enough halting English to greet Thomas. Simon couldn't understand a single word of the German except "ja," but he could tell they were having a good time.

The morning went swiftly. At lunch time, Simon went over to the bench as before and again picked up the *Daily*

Picayune. Friday was certainly an all-round better day. On the page where slaves had been advertised for sale on Thursday, this paper carried two columns of rewards for the capture and return of runaways—*so they did sometimes get away!* Simon particularly noted:

THREE HUNDRED DOLLARS REWARD

Ran away from the plantation of Mme Delhommer, on the night of the 23rd November last, the yellow man BOB. He is about 6 feet high, retreating forehead, full face, and has an impudent look....

Also black boy CHARLIE, rather spare built, quick spoken and intelligent; speaks English and French; is about 5 feet 6 inches high and about 18 years of age....

Simon was glad BOB had an impudent look and hoped both he and the intelligent CHARLIE got well out of reach.

*   *   *

After lunch, Thomas laid out the wooden wagon wheels that had been brought in the day before, then stood aside waiting for directions as Herr Grossmann called to Simon, "Come and watch, lad. This is an important job that goes much better with a helper. You'll see why."

First the smith laid a long iron rod on the anvil and took a tool from the rack, saying, "This is called a 'traveler.'" He then proceeded to walk slowly, methodically around the wagon wheel, pushing a smaller wheel with a handle while obviously counting. He wrote down some figures and then did it all over again. Seeing Simon's look of puzzlement he told him firmly:

"Never forget, son, always measure at least twice. It's the first law every workman has to learn, whether he's a smith or a carpenter or a tailor. If your measurements aren't right the whole job is wrong. Do you understand how the traveler works?"

"Not exactly."

"Well, it has a mark on it so you can tell when it has turned all the way around. On this wheel that circumference is six inches. I also marked a starting point on the wagon wheel and counted how many times the traveler revolved until I got it back where I began. That should be enough explanation for a lad like you that's supposed to be a dab at figures, is it?"

"Yes, sir, thank you."

After marking the iron rod, Herr Grossmann wrote some more numbers on paper, then used a small measure to place another mark an inch or so behind the first one. After that he picked up his short handled chisel and made a quick sharp cut at the second mark. Simon jumped. *Surely the iron was now too short to go around the wheel. What could the smith be thinking of?*

He managed to choke back his protest, but both men noticed and glanced his way, then went about their business without comment. Herr Grossmann heated the ends of the tire quickly and hammered each end so that its face sloped diagonally. He then picked up one end. Thomas took the other and the men stepped outside to the largest of the trees with a mystified Simon right behind. Saying, "watch," Herr

Grossmann placed his end against the tree; Thomas began bending the tire around it. They kept this up until they had created a rough circle.

Herr Grossmann, with Simon in tow, then took it inside and hammered it over the horn of the anvil until the circle was nearly perfect before welding the ends together. This was achieved by placing the tire on the forge with the ends in the fire and piling additional coal over them, then pumping the bellows slowly until welding heat was reached. Finally the smith placed the tire on the anvil and joined the ends with a few quick hammer blows. *Was he now going to find out that it was too small?*

Bearing the tire, the smith and his would-be apprentice stepped back out to the yard where Thomas had built a fire in a circle of stones. The wooden wheel lay on the millstone close by. Herr Grossmann put the tire into the fire and placed pieces of firewood over it, muttering over his shoulder to Simon, "Have to keep the heat even."

Simon was glad to be told something. He did now realize that the hot iron would stretch, but he was still worried. The smith watched the fire intently and periodically rubbed the iron with a small dry stick. The stick suddenly slid wildly as though it had been greased and a small curl of smoke rose from it. That was the signal. Thomas was ready with tongs and the two men lifted the tire and placed it over the wheel. Herr Grossmann then knocked it into place with a light sledge hammer.

BLACKSMITHING

The rim smoked and the joints of the wheel cracked and groaned. Simon had never imagined that a piece of wood could complain so loudly. Thomas poured cold water around the circumference as the cracking and groaning continued. Nothing broke, however, and when the wheel was finally quiet, Herr Grossmann addressed Simon:

"Well, lad, we're going to do this three more times. Try not to fret.

The tire absolutely *has* to fit tight enough to make the wheel groan or it won't stay on as it should. As an apprentice you'll need to trust my craft. Understand?"

"Oh, yes, sir. I'm sorry. I do trust your skill, but it was so surprising."

"No harm. You *do* pay attention. We might make a smith out of you one day."

Simon enjoyed his role of observer during the rest of the afternoon. He started to anticipate each step of the tire-making process and to feel knowledgeable, although he recognized that he wasn't quite ready to jump in and weld the tire ends together or hammer the red-hot tire onto the wheel himself!

Also, when several customers came in with tools to be mended, Herr Grossmann just said he'd get to them as soon as he could and referred them to his young clerk, who wrote down their names and identified what they were leaving.

Simon kept turning over in his mind that the smith had said *we* as though he and Thomas were already partners and talked about making *him*, Simon, into a smith as though he were already an apprentice. It was almost too good to be true.

This rosy prospect was reinforced at the end of the day when Herr Grossmann again spoke encouragingly to Simon:

"I understand, lad, that you and young Patrick are going to enjoy the sights of New Orleans tomorrow. While you're doing that, be sure to give full attention to the magnificent ironwork that is the city's glory."

With that he pulled a twenty-five cent piece out of his pocket and handed it to an overwhelmed Simon. "Have some of your good time on me. When you come back on Monday, if there's time, I think we'll get you started on a simple task like making pothooks— let you get the feel of a tool in your hand. Go along now."

"Oh, sir, thank you sir, I don't know what to say."

"Enough—just go."

Father and son did as they were told, both well satisfied with their day, and just before they reached the O'Malleys' Thomas produced a twenty-five cent piece of his own, which he handed to Simon saying,

"I don't want to be outdone by Herr Grossmann. Also, while I have no doubt that Patrick intends to treat you, I think it's much better for you to be able to pay your share. Right?"

"Oh yes, Da!

X

A Day in New Orleans

Simon and Patrick set out next morning for their day on the town, pleased with themselves and with the world. The sun shone brightly. A gentle breeze played around them, and everywhere they looked they saw flowers in profusion.

"Is the weather always perfect like this?" asked Simon.

Patrick laughed: "Much as I want you to love New Orleans, I can't tell you that. Quite soon now, it is going to get really hot and muggy. Then we will have beautiful weather again for a while until the rains. It doesn't get cold here in the winter. It just rains."

"It rains a lot in Ireland too."

"Yes, but it rains gently there. Here, the rain comes as a deluge and just keeps coming. It causes flooding. One of the sights of New Orleans is the St. Louis graveyard where all the tombs are above ground to keep bodies from being washed up in the rainy season, but what I want to show you today is a live town." Patrick then turned north away from the river:

"Since we are on holiday, we should see the sights in comfort. I think I'll treat us to a ride on the St. Charles streetcar."

"That's fine, but you don't have to treat. Herr Grossmann gave me a twenty-five cent piece to spend, and Da gave me another."

"Herr Grossmann made you a present of a twenty-five cent piece to spend today? Jesus, Mary and Joseph, he really likes you, Simon! You and your Da don't need to worry about your future. Let's have a high old time."

"That's fine with me."

The boys walked on companionably until they reached St. Charles Avenue, where Simon saw rails running down the center of the street. He peered up and down and was soon rewarded by the sight of two black mules pulling a car along the tracks. Neither they nor their driver seemed to be in any hurry! Patrick signaled the driver with a wave saying: "Let's get on here. This car will just take us to the end of the line and turn around. We can ride as long as we like for five cents apiece."

The driver obligingly pulled the mules to a stop so the two boys could board. They seated themselves happily on slatted wooden seats next to windows open to the world as the conveyance resumed its leisurely pace.

The car was about half full and had a holiday atmosphere about it since most of their fellow-passengers gave evidence of being sightseers too.

Simon leaned back, stretched his legs and gave himself up to comfort and pleasure. He couldn't remember ever having had a day quite like this. As Patrick had said, they soon came to the turnaround. A few passengers got off, several others got on, and then they headed toward the heart of New Orleans, its French Quarter.

On their way, the streetcar made its leisurely way past several large, handsome houses surrounded by a breathtakingly beautiful selection of flowering trees and shrubs. The mule driver responded to Simon's audible gasp:

"This is where rich Americans chose to settle after they purchased Louisiana. It's called the Garden District. You can see why. Some of us old-timers still prefer the French Quarter though."

They rode along until they reached Canal Street, after which St. Charles Avenue became Royal Street, where the two young holiday-makers disembarked to explore the part of New Orleans that the mule driver preferred.

As they walked along Royal Street they saw beautiful iron scrollwork on balcony after balcony. Even a short week of observation in a blacksmith's shop had provided Simon with a sense of what remarkable artistry and craftsmanship he saw on almost every building. Noticing how impressed his friend was, Patrick commented:

"You might be interested to know that most of this decorative ironwork was hammered out by Negro slaves in the workshops here. Some of them brought the skill with them from Africa.

"That's one way the French treated their slaves differently. The French encouraged them to use what talents they had and allowed them to earn money. The slaves didn't get to keep it all, but they kept some and were often able to use it to buy their freedom. That's one reason why New Orleans has so many free people of color."

The boys walked on, admiring the old buildings until Patrick said, "Now, down to Jackson Square. It's time to introduce you to the Hero of New Orleans and for us to have refreshments."

*   *   *

This was a puzzler for Simon, but he just kept still and waited for the answer. They reached the square in only a few minutes. It was filled with an assortment of people, but it was not so full that Simon failed to see its central feature—the statue of a soldier on horseback, confidently controlling a magnificent, rearing horse with one hand while tipping his hat to the crowd with the other.

"There he is," said Patrick, "General Andrew Jackson, the Hero of New Orleans."

"He certainly looks it, but how did he get to be the Hero of New Orleans?"

"Follow me to the café on the levee and I'll tell you."

Soon they were seated with cups of café au lait and a full plate of warm "beignets" to nibble on. These were feather-light French pastries covered with powdered sugar. Simon had never tasted anything like them. He tried hard not to gobble, but didn't quite succeed. Still, he did listen to Patrick:

"Andrew Jackson became the hero of New Orleans by defeating the English army in the battle of New Orleans at the end of the War of 1812—although a peace treaty had already been signed before the battle."

"Then why was Jackson such a hero?"

"Neither army knew about the treaty. The battle was bound to be fought. Jackson led the U.S. to its only major victory of the war and restored American national pride. He also made use of another famous New Orleans figure. Did you ever hear of Jean LaFitte?"

"No, should I have?"

"Well, he was a famous pirate who was also a blacksmith! Jackson found his lair and asked for help against the invading English army. LaFitte and his men fought bravely in defense of the city and were acclaimed as patriots even though they were law-breakers. Pirates Alley is named for them. Andrew Jackson went on to become a two-term President of the United States."

Simon took his eyes off the statue long enough to pay attention to the other customers of the café. Most of them seemed to be speaking French, a few English, but he heard many other languages he couldn't even guess at. Patrick thought he could identify both Spanish and Italian, but then gave up saying:

"You can hear just about anything here, Simon. The whole world comes to New Orleans."

Well, they were part of that world!

*   *   *

Full of delectable food and a sense of camaraderie, the two world citizens set off to see more of the sights of New Orleans. They walked first to the Old Ursuline Convent on Chartres Street, which was now the Bishop's residence. Patrick, in his role as guide, told Simon that this was the oldest building in the city; that twelve nuns had come from

France in 1723 to provide nursing and education for what was then only a settlement. The nuns had a new building now, because there were more of them and they were running an orphanage as well as nursing and educating the needy.

From there it was only a few blocks down Chartres to St. Louis Cathedral, a beautiful, historic church. Simon asked:

"How could the Ursuline Convent be older than the Cathedral?"

"Because a fire destroyed the original Cathedral and most of the rest of New Orleans, but spared the old Convent. You're quite right, the Bishop had a church before he sent a plea for help to the Ursulines and built a convent for them—enough of history, we're here for fun. Follow me around the corner, and let's see what's going on."

*   *   *

Simon obeyed his leader and was immediately dazzled by a variety of entertainers. First, he and Patrick joined the crowd around a juggler. Simon couldn't even count how many balls were in play because the juggler kept doing fantastic tricks amid oohs and aahs from the crowd even as he kept the balls aloft. It was breathtaking. Great applause greeted the end of his act. Some of the crowd tossed coins into his bowl and Patrick and Simon joined in.

They were in a sort of park behind the Cathedral where musicians, dancers and assorted performers presented themselves to an appreciative public. The boys rested a few minutes on a convenient bench to survey the scene. Food vendors came along purveying their wares. As everywhere in this city, people were laughing and talking in many languages. Simon was becoming less uncomfortable with this. He couldn't understand any of them, but they didn't seem unfriendly.

He and Patrick bought themselves pasties first and then sweets, but still had enough money to throw coins to the performers and feel like a pair of fine gentlemen. *God bless his Da and Herr Grossmann for their generosity.*

*   *   *

When they had had their fill of the entertainment, they wandered around some more, walked through Pirates Alley, looked in at the Courtyard of Two Sisters with its "charm gates" made in Spain and blessed by Queen Isabella, then stopped briefly at the Napoleon House. Patrick said this mansion had been prepared by a Mayor of New Orleans who plotted to free Napoleon from St. Helena and offer him sanctuary. (Napoleon died before that expedition could be mounted.)

*   *   *

Finally, they started up towards Royal Street to catch a ride home on the St. Charles streetcar. Their holiday mood changed abruptly as they came upon a group of miserable Negroes, dressed in black, being looked over and even poked at by assorted passersby. Simon almost cried out in protest. Patrick, also in distress, drew him quickly away:

"Oh, Simon, it is just what it looks like. Those are slaves for sale. They'll be taken inside shortly and auctioned off. I'm so sorry we had to see it just now. It *is* terrible. It's just as terrible as you think it is, but it's still true that there isn't anything you can do. Please, *please*, don't let it spoil our day!"

"All right, Patrick, I won't. New Orleans is a wonderful city in a lot of ways, and you have given me a grand treat. I won't forget it."

*　　　*　　　*

Simon was thoughtful on the ride home—Patrick had said much the same thing he'd said before—that there was nothing Simon could do about slavery, but it had sounded entirely different. He hadn't brushed Simon's worry aside or reminded him he was only twelve or told him not to be daft. Patrick was a real friend and he, Simon, was not going to let himself be offended again.

*　　　*　　　*

By the time the gadabouts got home the rest of the family had all had their Saturday-night baths and were ready for supper. Patrick and Simon ate with the others. They then made several trips to the cistern with water pitchers to fill the tub in the center of the room that Thomas and Martha shared with the younger boys. They scrubbed themselves well with soap and rinsed off with the cold water in preparation for Sunday. They didn't waste any time. It had been a long day.

As soon as they had emptied the tub, both of them fell onto their pallets, satisfied and weary, and slept deeply. Simon dreamed of riding a spirited horse into battle with Andrew Jackson on one side of him and Jean LaFitte on the other. As

Simon

he was about to clash head-on with murderous-looking English soldiers, he woke with a start, his heart pounding, but no one was there except a peacefully sleeping Patrick!

XI

Sunday

Morning entailed yet another expedition into New Orleans, this time to church. It was the first time for almost two months that the O'Sheas had had a chance to go to church. Simon found it very satisfying to be going with such a large family group. Agnes chose to remain at home with Maureen, saying:

"We're going to have a church here in Lafayette in another year or two and then we'll all be able to get to Mass every Sunday, but right now it's too far to take a baby. You'll like St. Pat's though."

Even so, it was a group of ten who set out briskly with Daniel in the lead. They were all in good spirits and without a barrow to push, or a baby to wheel, or any need to ask directions, it didn't seem long until they heard the sound of church bells.

Maggie burst out, "Are they ringing for *us*?"

"Yes, lass," said Daniel, "you're in America. All churches are welcome to call their worshippers to service. None are official and none are illegal. That's one big reason so many people are coming here."

In just a few minutes they started up the steps of Saint Patrick's along with a considerable crowd, a number of whom spoke to Daniel as they passed. Instead of all the foreign speech he had listened to yesterday, Simon heard nothing but English, spoken with the familiar brogue. Today, New Orleans seemed to be an Irish city, but one where bells rang in invitation to a beautiful church filled with light from its stained glass dome.

Yes, thought Simon, *in spite of slavery, I do really want to be an American, and I do like St. Pat's.*

After Mass they received greetings and encouragement from several friends of the O'Malleys, including the men they had queried about directions—*could it have been only last Tuesday?*—and the man they had talked to in the smithy. They didn't tarry long, however, as they had to make the walk back before they could satisfy their hunger with another of Agnes's meals. Since it was Sunday, she had fixed chicken and mashed potatoes and gravy. It was a real feast!

XII

Simon's First Try at Smithing

After his holiday, Simon arrived at the smithy Monday morning filled with anticipation. This would be his first step toward apprenticeship—unless Herr Grossmann had forgotten. If he did well, as he devoutly intended, perhaps signing of papers would be next.

As usual, six or seven horses and their owners were waiting in the courtyard, but with two smiths on duty the shoeing didn't take long. Then the moment came:

"Simon," Herr Grossmann called brusquely, "it's time for you to start making pothooks."

"Yes, sir, I'm ready."

"First watch me and then just do it. You don't have to measure for this job. You just need to develop an eye for the right length. Here we go."

*   *   *

The master smith stationed himself at the small anvil with some of the same iron rods he had used for the tires on Friday. He laid a rod on the anvil and made a quick cut. He then took the piece which Simon judged to be about six to eight inches long, bent one end around the horn of the anvil to make a hook, then bent the other in the opposite direction to form a slightly elongated S. The pothook was complete. It looked really easy.

"All right, lad, your turn."

*   *   *

Simon accepted the short-handled chisel from Herr Grossmann and made a somewhat hesitant attempt to cut about where he thought he should. The chisel didn't even go all the way through the rod. The smith took the cutting tool back and made another sharp cut saying, "If you're going to cut, *do* it. There's nothing to be afraid of."

Then, handing it back to Simon, "Cut again right now. Don't worry about where, just be quick and firm." Simon did as he was told.

"Again."

He did it again—and again—and again. Each time the chisel went through cleanly:

"All right. Now bend the end of one of those pieces."

Simon proved awkward at this too. He got the piece bent part way, but it slipped out of his hand while it was still a miserable excuse for a hook.

"Not quite as easy as it looks, is it? But you can do it. Watch me again. Hold the rod firm, like this, and bend it quickly."

Herr Grossmann's powerful hands held the iron against the horn, bending it smoothly and effortlessly. "You're strong enough. You just need practice. Keep going until you get it right, and then keep on until you fall into a rhythm. We can

always use a good supply of pothooks. I'll see to my customers now."

*   *   *

Simon noticed that several men had come into the store
and were conferring with Thomas. Blacksmith shops seemed
always to be busy. At least, this one did.

He turned to his own task. He managed to bend the end of
the rod, though not smoothly like the smith.

He had to make numerous attempts before he actually created a pothook. *Praise God neither Herr Grossmann nor his Da
had stood by to watch him fumble.*

*   *   *

Just as he was thinking this, commotion arose outside. A
man rushed in shouting, "There's fire on Camp Street. It
looks like a big one. They're sounding a general alarm."

Everybody left the shop and looked to the east where
smoke and flames were indeed visible, growing even as they
watched. Herr Grossmann said:

"Thomas, I think we must both go and see what help is
needed. Simon, stay put and mind the smithy. I doubt there'll
be much if any business. We'll be back before too long, God
willing. Just keep on doing what you're doing."

*   *   *

As temporary man-in-charge, Simon took a little time off
from his pothooks to stroll around. He examined the rows of
hammers and chisels, took some of them down and hefted

them. He recognized the light sledge hammer that the smith used to pound tires. He thought he could wield it with a little practice, but when he picked up the largest sledge, wondering what jobs it was for, he knew he was not yet ready for it.

Next, he looked over the array of punches and drilling tools. Both Herr Grossmann and his Da used the drills frequently. Of course, the smiths used them to make holes of different sizes, but Simon hadn't paid attention to the jobs they were using them for. So far, fitting horseshoes and making iron tires for wagon wheels were the only procedures he had observed intently. Now that he was really on his way, he resolved to watch and remember everything.

He glanced at the rack of specialized small tools from which Herr Grossmann had plucked the traveler, wondering how long it would take to learn all their names and what they were for. But, after his struggle with the pothooks, it occurred to him that the real question was: *How long would it take him to learn to actually use them?*

Before getting back to work, Simon stepped outside to see what he could of the fire. Smoke and flames still covered a large area. It was too far for him to see just what was going on, but he thought there was a considerable crowd. Nobody was on the street in Lafayette.

Laura Sheerin Gaus

POTHOOKS

XIII

Fire

Simon was right about the crowd. Herr Grossmann and Thomas had rushed to join a throng at the rapidly expanding inferno in a business section of the city. Noise and confusion threatened to overwhelm them. Intense heat poured from the burning buildings along with huge clouds of dark smoke reeking from the devastation within.

Someone called out, "Hans Grossmann, over here!" Gratefully, they joined a small group of men who told them what had happened so far. The fire had started in and totally destroyed a grocery store, then demolished a stationer's next door before spreading to an adjacent four-story structure with its large stock of rope and bagging.

They watched firemen working desperately to halt the relentless progress of devastation, but just as the efforts seemed to be succeeding, the wind changed; flames rushed down the street and shot up almost simultaneously from several buildings on the other side of the still-smoldering grocery store. Two of the buildings were tobacco warehouses. Workers began throwing out as many large sacks of tobacco as they could manage in an effort to save at least some of the stock before making their own desperate exit.

Confusion turned to chaos. A wild collection of looters rushed in, helping themselves to the tobacco and anything else that could be salvaged from the wreckage. A greatly out-numbered police force, wielding clubs and shouting for order, was inadequate to protect property or, even more important, keep the path clear for the firefighters. The noise of screams and curses in a variety of languages almost deafened the onlookers.

Now, the group of which the two blacksmiths were a part, along with a number of similar groups, all of them choking from the smoke, pushed their way into the maelstrom to stand shoulder to shoulder with the police. They didn't achieve anything like order, much less quiet, but they did manage to create enough space for the beleaguered firefighters to maneuver their wagons and direct the full force of their hoses against the conflagration.

Again, just as it seemed the battle might be won, another vagrant swirl of wind carried flames to the opposite side of the street. A new path had to be cleared, a new all-out war had to be fought against the destruction. Confusion became, if possible, greater than ever. An additional four buildings, one of them a cotton warehouse, exploded in flames. The cotton warehouse and an adjacent furniture store were consumed in minutes. The firemen, working heroically, managed to save most of the bank building, including the area where deposits were kept.

Finally, the battle ended in the four-story brick building of the *Daily Picayune*. The building was almost totally destroyed, but so was the fire. Just as a final wall fell to a watery grave, battle-scarred newsmen emerged triumphant with the rescue of one small press. The disorderly crowd began to disperse.

Thomas and Herr Grossmann started back to the smithy, pleased with the outcome and feeling no need to rush with the emergency behind them.

XIV

Crisis Time

While all the excitement was taking place on Camp Street, Simon had become quite proficient at making pothooks. Working by himself, with nobody to observe his awkwardness, he gradually overcame it. He just kept making sharp cuts with his chisel, followed by bending the little rods into elongated S shapes. He developed an increasing ease. Finally, he noticed with some astonishment that the rhythm Herr Grossmann had spoken of was now present in his work. He felt elevated almost to man's estate.

Flushed with pride, he stepped outside again to check the fire. It appeared to have diminished, so he quickly returned to his anvil, determined that the returning smiths should find him hard at work and in full control of his craft. He whistled as he went back to his labors. Life couldn't get much better than this!

★   ★   ★

Suddenly, strange sounds of clanking metal and shuffling feet interrupted his euphoria. As he looked up, the whole world changed. The horrifying figure of a wild-eyed black man, his legs shackled with irons, lurched into the shop and fell at Simon's feet. With clasped hands raised in the universal gesture of supplication he cried out, "For Gawd's sake, Massa!"

Simon had seen plenty of suffering in his native Ireland where men, women and children were on the brink of starvation, but this was the first time he had looked straight at the face of naked terror.

He hadn't been able to relieve the hunger of starving Irish children, or to do anything for the slave boy who had gazed at him so beseechingly, but now, he was standing alone at an anvil with a cutting tool in his hand. Almost mindlessly, he made two quick, clean strokes with his chisel and the leg irons fell away. The fugitive gave a heartfelt cry of thanksgiving and was out of the shop and running for his life.

*   *   *

He left behind a young boy almost as scared as he. Simon looked at the irons. *What would Herr Grossmann say or his father? Should he hide them? Could he pretend nothing had happened?* He knew he couldn't. He was trembling all over. Work was impossible. He threw the chains over against the forge and tried to get hold of himself.

Laura Sheerin Gaus

CHAINS

Before he could manage that, the two men appeared in the doorway. Herr Grossmann's gaze instantly riveted on the pieces of broken metal lying against his forge.

"Did you cut those off a slave?"

"Yes, sir."

Thomas stepped quickly to the side of his son. The two men exchanged a level look. Then:

"Thomas, there are boats leaving for the North at five o'clock this afternoon. You and your family are to be on one. I cannot be responsible for your lives or your safety."

The smith stepped to his money box:

"There is no time for talk. As we left the fire, I heard a man screaming that a slave had escaped. Sorry indeed I am to lose you both, but *you must not be found here.* Take this. Just go— and Godspeed."

*   *   *

In blind obedience to the urgency of the command, Father and son left the smithy, with Simon now nearly hysterical, "Oh, Da, I'm so sorry, but if you could have seen his face…"

"It's all right, son, you did what you had to do. We'll talk later. Now we must just hurry, and I must think what *I* need to do."

XV

Aftermath

The next few hours were a blur to Simon. He remembered getting back to the O'Malleys' and being amazed at the speed with which his mother and Mrs. O'Malley accepted the news and went to work. They neither reproached him nor asked any questions. (He would have understood this more easily if he could have seen the pallor of his own face.)

Somehow, the children were gathered in from their play. Belongings went back into carpet bags and knapsacks from which they had so recently emerged. Even excitable, talkative Maggie just went quietly to work, helped, of course, by Brigid. Agnes packed a hamper with bread and cheese and fruit for their journey.

His father came in with Daniel O'Malley. Thomas had found his old friend at work and they had been to the steamship line to book passage. Daniel put an arm around Simon, saying,

"You're a brave lad; I'm proud of you and sorry indeed that New Orleans has turned you into a fugitive."

"Daniel, would a young lad like Simon really receive harsh judgment in court?" asked Martha.

"No, it's not the court we have to worry about. It's an angry, vengeful slaveholder taking the law into his own hands. The police just look the other way in these cases. There's no telling what would happen to Simon. Hans Grossmann is absolutely right."

*   *   *

"The important thing is to stay calm and not call attention to your sudden departure. Are you pretty well packed?"

"Yes, we are. All the children have helped—even Maureen has managed to keep quiet."

Agnes, who had been bustling around the stove, interrupted here, "Since we have all worked so quickly, there is time for us to have a meal before they have to leave, is there not?"

"Indeed, there is. Patrick should join us any minute. I left him to complete a job that I'd promised for noon today. I didn't want any customers to get the impression of a crisis at our house."

Just as Daniel finished speaking, Patrick came through the door and headed straight for the white-faced Simon. Gripping him strongly on both arms, he said,

"What a lad you are! How could I have ever said there was nothing you could do? I'll *never* forget you. I am sure you are going to do *many* great things, and that somehow we will manage to meet again."

A little color returned to Simon's wan cheeks: "Oh, thank you, Patrick. I'm glad you don't think me a fool. You are the best friend I've ever had or ever could have, and since you believe we'll meet again I believe it too."

*   *   *

With that they all sat down for their last meal together. Daniel asked a blessing and Agnes said, "Eat heartily. It will need to last you for a while." They all fell to. Even Simon, who had thought he had no appetite, found that yesterday's reheated chicken and gravy tasted good and went down easily. He'd had a horrible fear that he might collapse before he got to the steamboat, but now he could feel strength returning. He didn't know it, but everybody at the table observed with relief that he was starting to look less like a ghost and more like himself again.

When they had all finished, Daniel spoke: "None of the O'Malleys are going to the levee with you. We don't want to encounter people we know who might ask questions. We will say our farewells here briefly. No weeping and wailing. Do you all understand?"

This injunction was hardest for Maggie and Brigid. They were hanging on tight to each other, but they nodded their heads along with the other children. They both had teary eyes, but they didn't actually weep, and they certainly didn't wail.

"All right, do whatever needs to be done, then gather at the door, so we can send you off with a blessing."

XVI

Northward Bound

In a few minutes the O'Shea family with all their luggage were in front of the house receiving their marching orders from Thomas:

"We're going back the way we came. Simon and I will again take turns wheeling the barrow. We don't want to call attention to ourselves in any way. Remember—just stay calm and stay together whatever happens, and we'll soon be safe aboard ship."

Then Daniel, with his family arrayed behind him, raised his hand in an Irish blessing:

"Go with God, dear friends. May the Blessed Mother and all the

angels and saints watch over you. May the road rise up to meet you and may the wind always be at your back – Farewell!"

*   *   *

With that all the O'Malleys stepped back and all the O'Sheas stepped forward. They were on their way again. Thomas and Martha led off. Kevin and John behind them, holding hands, followed by Simon pushing the barrow along with Maggie, who, with only a small shove and no words, had firmly taken her place at his side. Simon felt a sudden surge of affection for this little sister, who had so often bickered with him, but now, in an emergency and faced with separation from her dearest friend, chose this way to show solidarity with her big brother. *Perhaps, all would yet be well.*

The small cavalcade moved much more rapidly than they had on their incoming trip. *Could it have been only a week ago?* This time they knew the way and no one felt like talking or asking any questions. Even five-year-old Kevin seemed to understand that that would all come later. After about twenty minutes, Thomas called a halt for regrouping:

"You're all doing fine, just keep it up. I'm going to push the barrow now because I don't want Simon doing it for the whole trip, even if he does have Maggie to help him, and when we get close to the levee, I want to be in the lead. I know exactly where we're going and just what we are to do. All right, let's proceed. Simon and Maggie, step in behind your Ma."

As they took their places, Simon said softly, "You're a grand help, Mag."

"Proud I am, indeed, that you should have noticed it," retorted his sister.

Simon laughed, much to his own astonishment. Martha gave a glad backward glance and the whole procession moved along more jauntily.

*   *   *

Simon

During the first part of the journey they had passed mostly horse-drawn wagons and only occasional pedestrians. Now the traffic began to get heavier and the variety of languages characteristic of New Orleans began to bombard them all.

Simon noted the approach of one sizable group of men, jabbering excitedly to each other in English. When they came close enough for him to hear what they were saying, he felt a rush of blood to his head and he almost stopped breathing:

"Andrews has not yet caught his slave that escaped during the fire."

"I heard the man had run away before. He was in irons."

"Then, how could he possibly get away?"

"Some cursed abolitionist must have helped him. Andrews is out for blood."

*　　　　*　　　　*

Simon's own pounding blood quieted a little as he heard his father say in perfectly ordinary tones, "We're almost there. Take the barrow now, lad, so I can lead us to the ship." Simon noted that his father had avoided using his name, but he did as he was told, looking neither to right nor left, and the family moved on. Nobody paid them the slightest attention. The whole terrifying episode was over in two to three minutes.

*　　　　*　　　　*

Wordlessly, the O'Sheas continued their journey at a steady pace and soon saw the parade of huge river boats pulled up at the dock with their tall chimneys sending out smoke and fire.

The crowded dock presented a scene of furious activity and earsplitting noise even more intense than they had seen on their arrival. Thomas, who had come this way less than two hours before, finally spoke:

"You're looking at the commerce of a nation. All these ships with cargo from the North and East have been unloaded and are now being reloaded with cargo from the South, and must be on their way back to the North in less than two hours.

"Our ship will be the first one out. We're heading for it now. Simon and Maggie can keep pushing the barrow, and the rest of us must hold tight to each other as we make our way through this throng. Here we go!"

*　　　　*　　　　*

It wasn't easy. Along with hundreds of other travelers, they had to make their way past a crew of men hurling freight barrels and huge sacks to another crew on shipboard. Both teams moved at top speed, screaming at each other at the top of their lungs, while yet others bellowed commands at the crowd, who could scarcely obey. They were having trouble moving at all.

Simon

TOWARD THE STEAMBOAT

Simon kept his eyes fixed on Thomas making slow progress, but shepherding his weary band successfully past all obstacles. Finally, they all arrived at the boarding gate.

In just a few minutes the last of the cargo was safely stowed and the welcome call came, "All aboard, step lively, all aboard." Thomas led his family onto the upper deck and found a place where they could spread their blanket. No vengeful pursuers had yet appeared, but the shouting and screaming on the dock kept suspense alive.

At last! The whistles blew, the paddlewheels turned, the crew cast off. The O'Sheas, out of immediate danger, were on their way into another great unknown.

*   *   *

Simon, still in shock, went to the rail and stood watching by himself until they were well away. Then he felt a warm, familiar hand on his shoulder.

"Well, son…"

"Oh, Da, this is all my fault. I've caused so much trouble. I will make it up to you. I promise."

"Nay, Simon, you have nothing to make up for. It cannot be wrong to save a man. You're a broth of a boy. I'm proud of what you did."

"Would you have done it, Da?"

"I don't know, son. No one knows how he will respond to a crisis until it comes upon him, but you carry my blood and you've had my teaching. I expect you did what your father would have done. I hope so."

"Thanks, Da, but where are we going and how are we going to manage?"

"We're going north, away from slavery. More than that I don't yet know. I'm going to pick up what information I can during the voyage, and we're going to put our trust in the Lord. It may be hard, but we are going to manage and we'll be all right. Can't you feel a small wind at your back?"

INDIANA

Epilogue

Thus ends the story of Simon's first week in America. Just as Patrick prophesied, Simon went on to do many things and was able to contribute substantially to his adopted country.

During the voyage up the Mississippi, Thomas made friends with a man from Ohio who advised the O'Sheas to debark at Cincinnati and accompany him to Dayton. Simon served his apprenticeship there while also educating himself in as many other ways as possible. When he was eighteen, he struck out on his own for a railroad town, Logansport, Indiana, to pursue a more varied career (the rest of the family soon followed). It was as a "Gentleman from Indiana" that he made his mark: newspaper editor, elected official, Democratic National Committee- man, entrepreneur....

When Simon finally revisited New Orleans some fifty years later, the *Daily Picayune* greeted him with the front-page headline:

PROMINENT MIDWESTERN BUSINESSMAN AND
POLITICAL LEADER VISITS NEW ORLEANS

It must have given him great satisfaction!

About the Author

Laura Gaus, a lifelong resident of Indianapolis, is a graduate of Connecticut College with an MA from Rutgers University. Now a widow, she has three sons, five grandsons and one granddaughter. She is also an experienced teacher and writer. The teaching came first—seven years of history and humanities at Indianapolis public high schools, followed by ten years of English and philosophy at Park-Tudor, a private college-preparatory school.

After that, she turned herself into a writer. Published works include numerous articles, mostly concerned with the arts, and several books: two well received local histories, *Shortridge High School 1864–1981, Ivy Tech—The First Twenty-Five Years* and, with Sara Buchwald, *Writing Your Memoirs,* a workbook for memoir writers and family historians.

Of recent years she has combined her two avocations to help several hundred students chronicle personal and family histories (some of which have led to publication). A number of Indiana libraries are now using her workbook as a basis for their writing classes. Of course, this has sparked an intense interest in her own family's history, particularly that of her Irish ancestors who fled their famine-stricken homeland in 1849. The dramatic tale of their first week in this country cried out to be presented imaginatively.

So, here is *SIMON,* her first work of fiction.

Notes

SIMON is exciting reading. The O'Shea family arrive in New Orleans in 1849. The setting is so richly and accurately detailed that there is a historical authenticity to the novel. One can see, hear, almost taste the melting pot of America. The plot is well paced, the characters are real and believable. Like Huck Finn, Simon experiences a crisis of conscience when he faces the moral blot on America, slavery. The way he faces his fateful encounter with a runaway slave propels the plot to its stirring conclusion.

Mary Golichowski Library/Media Specialist, Park-Tudor School, Indianapolis, IN

SIMON is a gem. It is historical fiction with all the necessary ingredients that teachers look for when selecting literature for classroom use. Anybody of almost any age would enjoy this book, but it gets my recommendation for history and English classes at the middle school level. Believable characters, realistic history and challenging vocabulary plus many avenues for student discussion make SIMON an excellent read. SIMON definitely would enhance the curriculum.

Betty Whittaker English and Latin Teacher, Carmel Middle School. Carmel, IN

Laura Gaus paints a vivid picture of New Orleans in the mid-1800s, and sets in it the engaging Simon O'Shea, who arrives with his Irish family to seek a better life. Young readers

Simon

will enjoy this excellent story in which Simon grapples with the reality of slavery in this new world and, doing so, takes his first long step toward manhood.

Barbara Shoup Novelist and Teacher, Broad Ripple High School, Indianapolis, IN